This book belongs to:

_____

_____

_____

W9-ASM-170

To Lili, my little sun
To Jeremy

Hachette Book Group • 1290 Avenue of the Americas, New York, NY 10104 • Visit us at LBYR.com • Originally published by Hachette Enfants/Hachette Livre in France as *Les émotions de Gaston—Je suis triste* © Hachette Livre / Hachette Enfants, 2018 • First U.S. Edition: January 2020 • Little, Brown and Company is a division of Hachette Book Group, Inc. • The Little, Brown name and logo are trademarks of Hachette Book Group, Inc. • The publisher is not responsible for websites (or their content) that are not owned by the publisher. • Library of Congress Cataloging-in-Publication Data Names: Chien Chow Chine, Aurélie, author, illustrator. • Title: Little Unicorn is sad / Aurélie Chien Chow Chine. • Other titles: Les émotions de Gaston - Je suis triste. English • Description: First U.S. edition. | New York : Little, Brown and Company, 2020. | Originally published in France by Hachette Enfants/Hachette Livre in 2018 under title: Les émotions de Gaston - Je suis triste. | Summary: A little unicorn feels all kinds of emotions, including sadness, and uses a breathing exercise to calm down. • Identifiers: LCCN 2018060500| ISBN 9780316531900 (hardcover) | ISBN 9780316531894 (ebook) | ISBN 9780316531887 (library edition ebook) • Subjects: | CYAC: Sadness—Fiction. | Breathing exercises—Fiction. | Unicorns—Fiction. • Classification: LCC PZ7.1.C4978 Lj 2020 | DDC [E]—dc23 | LC record available at https://lccn.loc.gov/2018060500 • ISBNs: 978-0-316-53190-0 (hardcover), 978-0-316-53193-1 (ebook), 978-0-316-53189-4 (ebook), 978-0-316-53191-7 (ebook) • PRINTED IN CHINA • APS • 10 9 8 7 6 5 4 3 2 1

Little Unicorn IS SAD

Aurélie Chien Chow Chine

L B

LITTLE, BROWN AND COMPANY

NEW YORK   BOSTON

This is Little Unicorn.
He is very much like all the other little unicorns....

Sometimes, **Little Unicorn** is happy.
Sometimes, he is **not** happy.
Sometimes, he is sad.
Sometimes, he is scared.
Sometimes, he is angry.

These are emotions.

And **Little Unicorn** feels all kinds of emotions.
Just like you.

But there is something that makes **Little Unicorn** special:
He has a **magical mane**!

When all is well, his mane shines
with the colors of the rainbow.

But when all isn't well, his mane changes...
and its color shows just what he feels.

Happy

Jealous

Angry

Guilty

Shy

Scared

Stubborn

Sad

How does **Little Unicorn** feel today?

Bad!

He feels gray in his heart,
and he's going to tell us why.

And you, how do you feel today?

Great

Good

Fine

Not good

Bad

Awful

Now, why does **Little Unicorn** feel
so terrible today?

Most of the time, he's a very happy little unicorn
who loves to spend time with his friends,
Eugene and Marie.

They always play together on the playground.

But today, **Little Unicorn**
doesn't agree with his friends.

Eugene and Marie want to play tag.
Little Unicorn wants to play ball.

They argue.

Eugene and Marie leave to play tag together.

Little Unicorn is left alone with his ball.

And all day long, **Little Unicorn** feels sad.

That night, **Little Unicorn** is still thinking about the argument with his two friends. It's troubling him.

He feels very sad.

So very sad!

It feels like he has a giant gray cloud in his head.
A cloud filled with rain.

What if, instead of waiting for the cloud to go away,
he could chase it away?

He can!

And when you feel a cloud of sadness inside,
you can do this **breathing exercise** to blow it away, too.

Breathing exercise
to blow away
the cloud of sadness

1 **Little Unicorn** closes his eyes.
He imagines the giant rain cloud in his head.
He breathes in through his mouth and
fills his belly.

2 **Little Unicorn** holds his breath. He holds his nose and thinks about his cloud.

3 **Little Unicorn** blows out very hard through his nose. He blows away his rain cloud of sadness!

Little Unicorn does this exercise **three times**.

It takes at least **three breaths**
to blow away the last of the raindrops!

At last, he begins to breathe normally.
Now that he's chased away the clouds from his head,
the **beautiful sun** can shine in.

Ah, **Little Unicorn** feels much calmer.
He's not upset with his friends anymore.

His good mood is back, and
the rainbow has returned to his mane.

If you use your breathing
to replace a cloud with the sun,
you'll feel much better, too.
And your **smile** will return!

Don't miss these other stories about
Little Unicorn!

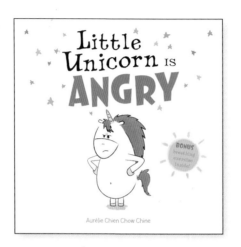

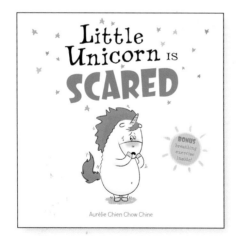

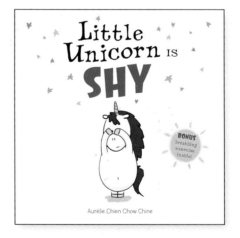

Available now!